THE UNLIKELY LOVEBIRDS

A LOVE STORY OF TWO CULTURES

PARTHASARATHY G

Copyright © Parthasarathy G
All Rights Reserved.

This book has been self-published with all reasonable efforts taken to make the material error-free by the author. No part of this book shall be used, reproduced in any manner whatsoever without written permission from the author, except in the case of brief quotations embodied in critical articles and reviews.

The Author of this book is solely responsible and liable for its content including but not limited to the views, representations, descriptions, statements, information, opinions and references ["Content"]. The Content of this book shall not constitute or be construed or deemed to reflect the opinion or expression of the Publisher or Editor. Neither the Publisher nor Editor endorse or approve the Content of this book or guarantee the reliability, accuracy or completeness of the Content published herein and do not make any representations or warranties of any kind, express or implied, including but not limited to the implied warranties of merchantability, fitness for a particular purpose. The Publisher and Editor shall not be liable whatsoever for any errors, omissions, whether such errors or omissions result from negligence, accident, or any other cause or claims for loss or damages of any kind, including without limitation, indirect or consequential loss or damage arising out of use, inability to use, or about the reliability, accuracy or sufficiency of the information contained in this book.

Made with ♥ on the Notion Press Platform
www.notionpress.com

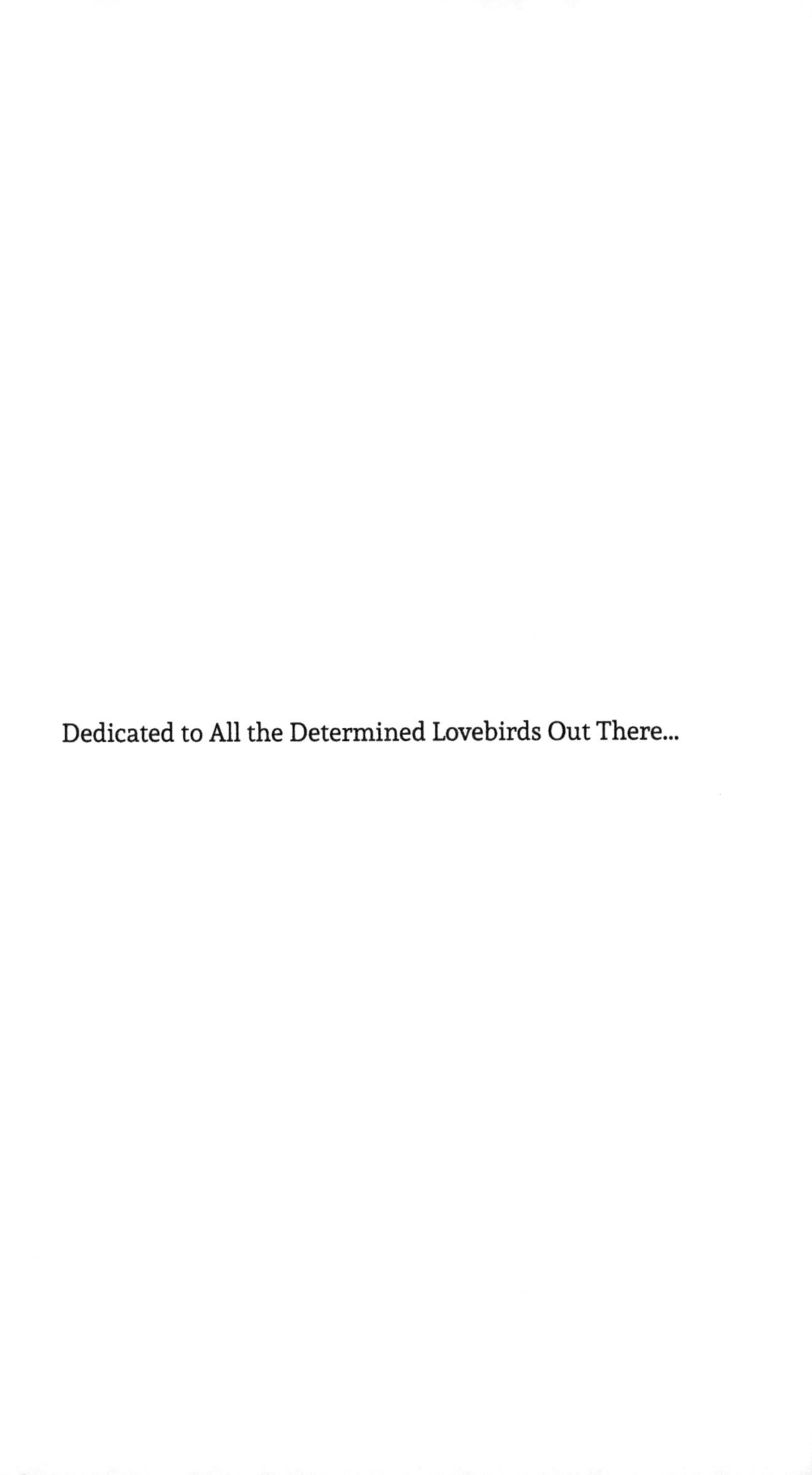

Dedicated to All the Determined Lovebirds Out There...

Contents

Acknowledgements *vii*

Prologue *ix*

1. Rohit: Dedicated And Persistent Boy 1
2. New Horizons: Rohit's Journey Through College 4
3. Leaving Home, Chasing Dreams: Rohit's Journey To The City 8
4. The Road To The Uk: Rohit's Adventure Abroad 11
5. Sarah's World: A Road To Self-discovery 15
6. Rohit's Rise In The Uk : Journey To Success 18
7. Romeo Meets Juliet: Love At First Sight 21
8. Love In The London City: Rohit And Sarah's Romantic Days 26
9. Disapproval And Heartbreak: Sarah's Parents' Reaction To Her Love 30
10. Rohit Breaking The News: Tells His Parents About Sarah And Love 34
11. The Battle For Love: Rohit's Struggle To Win Over Sarah's Parents 38
12. First Impressions: Sarah Meets Rohit's Parents 41
13. Bridging The Gap: The Meeting Of Rohit And Sarah's Families 44
14. The Engagement: A Celebration Of Love 48
15. Wedding Bells In India: A Union Of Two Cultures 51
16. A New Beginning: Life After Marriage 56

Contents

Epilogue 59

The Unlikely Lovebirds: A Love Story Of Two Cultures 61

Stay Connected: Follow The Author On Social Media 63

Acknowledgements

Thank you, dear reader and friend, for choosing to read "The Unlikely Lovebirds: A Love Story of Two Cultures".
I would like to express my gratitude to everyone who supported me in writing this book.
First and foremost, I would like to thank Lucky, my first reader, for her invaluable feedback.

I would also like to thank my friends and family who have made life worth living. A special shoutout to my extended family on Instagram, Twitter, and Facebook for their constant support.

Last but not least, I want to express my appreciation to the entire team at NotionPress Publications for their hard work in bringing this book to life.

Welcome to "The Unlikely Lovebirds: A Love Story of Two Cultures". I hope you enjoy reading it as much as I enjoyed writing it.

Prologue

It was a sunny afternoon in London, and the air was filled with the sweet fragrance of spring flowers. The city was bustling with life, as people rushed to and fro, going about their daily routines. But in a small corner of the city, in a cozy cafe, something special was happening.

It was the 25th anniversary of Rohit and Sarah, a couple who had defied all odds and proven that love knows no boundaries. And their son Raj was there, sitting at a table with a group of his friends, telling them the story of his parents' love.

Raj had always known that his parents were different from other couples. They had a bond that was unbreakable, a love that was pure and true. And as he recounted the story of how they had met, how they had fallen in love, and how they had overcome countless obstacles, his friends listened in awe.

Raj started with the moment when his father, Rohit, had arrived in London for his job as an engineer. He talked about how his father had always dreamed of seeing the world and how he had worked hard to make that dream come true. And then he told them about the fateful day when his parents had met in a art gallary, and how that chance encounter had changed their lives forever.

As Raj spoke, the cafe around them seemed to fade away, and his friends were transported to a different time and place. They saw the young Rohit and Sarah, lost in conversation, their eyes filled with wonder and hope. They heard the music that had played in the background, the laughter that had filled the air, and the whispers of destiny that had brought them together.

And as Raj continued his tale, he told them about the challenges that his parents had faced. He spoke of the cultural differences that had threatened to tear them apart, the doubts that had crept into their minds, and the moments when they had almost given up. But he also talked about the strength of their love, the courage of their hearts, and the unwavering faith that had kept them going.

As Raj finished his story, his friends applauded, moved by the power of his parents' love. And as he looked around, he saw the pride and joy on his parents' faces, knowing that their love had inspired not just their son but an entire generation.

For Rohit and Sarah, their love story had been a journey filled with drama, tears, and laughter. But it had also been a testament to the human spirit, to the beauty of diversity, and to the magic of love. And on their 25th anniversary, as they looked into each other's eyes, they knew that their love would last forever, a flame that would never die.

"Dear reader, as we embark on this journey together, let us turn the page and delve deeper into the captivating story of ***"The Unlikely Lovebirds : A Love Story of Two Cultures"****. Let us unravel the mysteries, experience the joys and sorrows, and witness the unforgettable moments that await us in the pages ahead. So come, let us explore this tale in all its richness and beauty.*

*Join us as we uncover the secrets of **'The Unlikely Lovebirds: A Love Story of Two Cultures.'"...***

♡♡♡

ONE

ROHIT: DEDICATED AND PERSISTENT BOY

Rohit was born in a small village in India, where he lived with his parents and two younger siblings. His father was a graduate but chose to become a farmer and his mother was a homemaker. Despite their humble beginnings, Rohit's parents were hardworking and dedicated, and they instilled the same values in their children.

Like every other child, to Rohit, his father was a source of inspiration and a reminder of the importance of education and hard work.

Growing up, Rohit was always fascinated by the world outside his village. He would spend hours reading books and magazines, and dreaming of one day traveling the world and experiencing new cultures. His parents encouraged his love for learning and education, and he was always one of the top students in his class.

Despite their best efforts, Rohit's family struggled to make ends meet. His father worked long hours on their farm, but the yield was often poor due to the dry and arid climate. Rohit's mother did her best to stretch their budget, but there was never enough money to go around.

Rohit often missed classes to help out on the farm. His education suffered, but Rohit was determined to succeed. He spent every spare moment reading books and teaching himself about the world beyond his village.

One day, as Rohit was studying for his engineering entrance exams, his mother walked into his room and asked, "What are you doing, Rohit?"

"I am studying for my engineering exams, Mom. I want to become an engineer and build things that will help people," Rohit replied, looking up from his books.

"Engineering? That sounds like a big dream, Rohit. But how will we afford your education?" his mother said, with a tone of concern in her voice.

Rohit replied, "I know it's not going to be easy, but I am determined to work hard and get a scholarship. I want to make you and Dad proud."

Despite the challenges they faced, Rohit's family was close-knit and loving. They would spend evenings together, playing games and telling stories. Rohit was particularly close to his mother, who encouraged him to pursue his dreams and never give up.

With the support of his family, Rohit continued to study hard and excel in his academics. He earned top grades in his school.

As Rohit got older, he started to help his father on the farm. He was a quick learner, and soon he was able to take on more responsibility. Despite the hard work, he loved being outdoors and working with his hands. He also appreciated the time he was able to spend with his father, who was his role model and best friend.

However, Rohit's dreams of traveling the world and experiencing new cultures never faded. He worked hard in school, and eventually he was accepted into a university in the city. This was a big opportunity for Rohit, and he was determined to make the most of it.

In the end, Rohit realized that his success was not just his own, but also a result of the love and support of his family and community. He was grateful for the opportunities he had been given and vowed to use his talents to make a positive impact in the world.

TWO

New Horizons: Rohit's Journey through College

Rohit's college life was a story of hard work, determination, and perseverance. Despite the obstacles he faced, Rohit was determined to make the most of his college experience and to get the best education possible.

One of the biggest challenges that Rohit faced was paying for his college education. As a student from a low-income family, he knew that it would be difficult to finance his education, but he was determined to make it work.

One day, as he was walking to his class, his friend Arjun asked him, "Hey Rohit, how's college life treating you?"

Rohit let out a sigh and replied, "It's been tough, to be honest. My family is struggling to pay for my fees, and I am working part-time to make ends meet."

Arjun nodded sympathetically and said, "I know how you feel, man. But don't worry, things will get better. You are one of the brightest students in our class, and I am sure you'll get a scholarship soon."

Rohit smiled and thanked Arjun for his support. He continued to study hard and excelled in his academics, often staying up late to prepare for exams.

At first, Rohit tried to work part-time jobs to help pay for his tuition and other expenses, but it was difficult to balance his studies and work. Despite this, he refused to give up, and he continued to look for ways to pay for his education.

Finally, Rohit found a solution. He learned about a scholarship program for students from low-income families, and he applied.

One day, he received the news that he had been awarded a scholarship. Overjoyed, he called his parents to share the good news.

His mother couldn't contain her happiness and said, "That's great news, beta! We are so proud of you. You have worked so hard to get this."

With the scholarship, Rohit was able to pay for his education without having to work part-time jobs. And focus more on his studies and perform even better.

With the financial burden lifted, Rohit was able to focus on his studies and to pursue his passion for learning. He threw himself into his classes, and he quickly became known as one of the top students in his program.

His professors were impressed by his dedication and by his natural talent, and they encouraged him to apply for research opportunities and other programs that would help him to further his education.

Rohit took their advice, and he soon found himself working on cutting-edge research projects alongside some of the best minds in his field. He was challenged and inspired, and he worked harder than ever before.

He became one of the toppers in his class and was offered a job by a top IT company even before he had completed his degree.

As graduation day approached, Rohit was filled with a sense of pride and accomplishment. He had come so far, and he had overcome so many obstacles, and now he was about to receive his degree and take the next step in his life.

When the day finally arrived, Rohit was filled with a sense of excitement and nervousness. He walked across the stage to receive his college degree, and as he did, he felt a wave of emotions wash over him. He had done it! He had graduated with flying colors, and he had accomplished something that he had never thought possible.

His parents were beaming with pride as they watched their son receive his degree. Rohit thanked his parents for their unwavering support and encouragement throughout his college years.

As the family embraces in a moment of pure joy, they are reminded of the power of hard work, dedication, and love.

After the ceremony was over, Rohit was surrounded by his friends and family, who were all proud of him and his achievements. He received congratulations from his professors and from the people who had helped him along the way.

As he walked out of the convocation hall, Rohit felt a sense of accomplishment and gratitude for the people who had helped him along the way. He knew that the road ahead would not be easy, but he was ready to face any challenges that lay ahead.

His story was a testament to the power of hard work, determination, and perseverance. He had faced many challenges, but he had never given up, and he had never lost sight of his goals.

From struggling to pay his fees to becoming a top performer, Rohit's college life had been a rollercoaster of emotions and challenges. But through it all, he had remained focused on his goals and had emerged stronger and more determined than ever before.

Rohit's college life ended in a great way. He faced many challenges and worked hard to overcome them. His success story will inspire many people in the future, and people will remember it for a long time. Rohit proved that with determination and hard work, anything is possible, even things that seem impossible. His story is a shining example of hope and perseverance, and it will continue to inspire others for years to come.

THREE

Leaving Home, Chasing Dreams: Rohit's Journey to the City

A small, humble house in a remote Indian village. The family is gathered together, preparing to bid farewell to their beloved son, Rohit, who is leaving for the city to join in his new job.

As Rohit bids farewell to his family, the air is filled with mixed emotions - sadness at his departure, pride at his achievements, and hope for his future. For this small village family, Rohit's departure is bittersweet. On the other hand, as they watch him disappear down the dusty village road, they are filled with hope for a better future, not just for Rohit, but for the entire family. And as they watch him go, they know that he carries with him the hopes and dreams of everyone he leaves behind.

Rohit's first job was a turning point in his life. After years of hard work and dedication, he was finally able to enter the workforce and start making a difference in the world.

However, the transition from student life to working life was not an easy one. Rohit found himself facing new challenges and obstacles, and he was quickly overwhelmed by the fast pace of city life.

One of the biggest challenges that Rohit faced was the sense of isolation that came with living and working in a big city. He missed the close-knit community of his hometown, and he struggled to make new friends and find a sense of belonging in his new environment.

On his first day at work, he woke up early, dressed in his best suit, and headed to the office. As he walked into the building, he was nervous but excited at the same time.

When he reached his desk, he was introduced to his team and given a brief on his trainings and job responsibilities. He was assigned to work on a new project, and he felt a rush of adrenaline as he thought about the impact he could make.

As the days went by, Rohit settled into his new job and started to get the hang of things. He worked long hours and put in extra effort to make sure that his work was of high quality.

One day, his boss called him into his office and said, "Rohit, I just wanted to tell you that you have been doing an excellent job. You are a quick learner, and your work has been outstanding."

Rohit felt a surge of pride as he heard those words. He knew that his hard work was paying off and that he was making a difference in his job.

As he continued to work in the company, Rohit made many new friends and learned a lot from his colleagues. He also started to explore the city in his free time, trying out new restaurants, and attending cultural events.

One day, as he was walking through the city, he saw a group of children playing in a park. He remembered his own childhood and how he had struggled to get an education. He decided that he wanted to do something to help these children.

With the support of his colleagues, he started a charity program to provide educational materials and support to underprivileged children in the city. The program was a huge success, and it helped hundreds of children get a better education.

Looking back on his first job, Rohit felt grateful for the experience and the opportunities it had given him. He had grown both professionally and personally, and he had made a positive impact in the world.

FOUR

THE ROAD TO THE UK: ROHIT'S ADVENTURE ABROAD

Rohit had always dreamed of going abroad to further his career. He had heard about the opportunities available in the United Kingdom, and he had set his sights on making it there one day.

One day, as he was working in his office, his boss called him into his office. "Rohit, I have some exciting news for you," his boss said with a smile.

"What is it?" Rohit asked, his heart racing with anticipation.

"You have been selected for a special project, and it's based in the United Kingdom!" his boss exclaimed.

Rohit's eyes widened with shock and excitement. "The UK? Really?" he exclaimed.

"Yes, really," his boss confirmed. "It's a big opportunity for you, Rohit. You'll be working on a high-profile project with some of the best professionals in the industry."

Rohit was over the moon. He had worked hard to get where he was, and he knew that this opportunity could be a game-changer for his career.

However, when a new opportunity arose for him to work in the UK, he found himself facing a difficult decision. On one hand, he was eager to explore a new culture and experience a new way of life. On the other hand, he was deeply rooted in his hometown and he did not want to leave behind the close relationships that he had built there.

Despite the conflicting emotions, Rohit felt drawn to the opportunity in the UK. He recognized that it was a once-in-a-lifetime chance to work for a well-respected company, and he knew that it would be an opportunity for him to grow both professionally and personally.

The next few weeks were a blur of activity for Rohit as he prepared to move to the UK. He had to apply for a visa, find a place to live, and make sure that all his paperwork was in order.

With a heavy heart, Rohit said goodbye to his friends and family and set off for the UK.

As he boarded the plane to the UK, Rohit felt a sense of excitement and trepidation. He was leaving behind everything he knew and loved for a new adventure in a foreign country.

The journey was long and tiring, but he was filled with a sense of excitement and anticipation as he stepped off the plane and made his way to his new home.

When he arrived in the UK, he was greeted by his colleagues, who made him feel welcome and at home. They showed him around the city and introduced him to the culture and customs of the country.

In the UK, Rohit was struck by the contrast between the fast-paced city life and the peaceful simplicity of his hometown. He was amazed by the sights and sounds of the bustling metropolis, and he was eager to explore the rich cultural heritage of the country.

However, despite the excitement, Rohit was also faced with the challenges of adapting to a new culture and way of life. He missed the familiarity of his hometown and the closeness of his friends and family, and he struggled to make new connections in his new environment.

Despite these challenges, Rohit threw himself into his work and quickly made a name for himself as a dedicated and hardworking employee. He was amazed by the opportunities that were available to him in the UK, and he was inspired by the innovative and forward-thinking approach of his colleagues.

As the months went by, Rohit found himself gradually becoming more and more comfortable in his new surroundings. He made new friends, discovered new interests, and learned to appreciate the unique qualities of the UK.

Despite his growing sense of belonging, however, Rohit never forgot his roots. He remained connected to his friends and family back home, and he took every opportunity to share the rich cultural heritage of his homeland with his new friends in the UK.

In the end, Rohit realized that his journey to the UK had been a transformative experience. He had grown both professionally and personally, and he had discovered a new appreciation for the rich cultural diversity of the world.

As he looked back on his journey, Rohit was filled with a sense of pride and gratitude. He had overcome the challenges of adapting to a new culture and way of life, and he had forged new relationships that would last a lifetime.

Rohit's journey was a reminder of the importance of embracing new opportunities, of staying connected to our roots, and of never losing sight of the things that truly matter in life.

FIVE

Sarah's World: A Road to Self-Discovery

Sarah was born in a small town in the United Kingdom, where she lived with her parents and two younger brothers. Her father was a businessman and her mother was a stay-at-home mom. They were a close-knit family and spent a lot of time together, playing games and going on trips.

Sarah's parents were very strict and conservative, with a strong focus on tradition and social status. They had high expectations for their daughter's education and future, often placing heavy pressure on her to succeed. They were also very particular about Sarah's social life, carefully monitoring her interactions with friends and potential romantic partners. Sarah often felt suffocated by their expectations and longed for a life of freedom and independence.

Growing up, Sarah was always a curious and adventurous child. She was fascinated by different cultures and would often spend hours reading books and watching documentaries about far-off places. Eventhough her parents were strict and conservative they encouraged her love for travel and learning, and would take her on trips to different parts of the UK and Europe.

Despite their comfortable lifestyle, Sarah's parents were hardworking and dedicated, and instilled the same values in their children. They encouraged Sarah and her brothers to work hard and pursue their passions, regardless of the challenges they might face.

Sarah excelled in school, and was always one of the top students in her class. She had a natural talent for languages, and soon became fluent in French, Spanish, and German. She also had a passion for art, and would spend hours drawing and painting.

As Sarah got older, she started to explore her interests in travel and art. She took trips to different parts of Europe, and spent time studying art in museums and galleries. Despite her busy schedule, she remained focused and determined, and was soon offered a admission to study art in college.

Despite the challenges she faced, Sarah thrived in college. She was surrounded by like-minded individuals who shared her passion for art, and she was able to develop her skills and knowledge. After graduation, she was offered a job in a top gallery in London, where she was able to put her education and experience to work.

However, Sarah was not content to just settle into her new job. She was always eager for new adventures and experiences, and soon she was traveling the world, visiting new places and meeting new people. She was able to use her talents as an artist to document her travels, and her work soon became popular among collectors and art lovers.

Despite her success, Sarah remained humble and grateful. She never forgot her roots, and would often return to her hometown to spend time with her family. She was a dedicated daughter, sister, and friend, and was always there for the people she loved.

As Sarah continued her travels, she encountered many challenges and obstacles, but she remained determined and resilient. She never lost her love for adventure and discovery, and was always eager to take on new challenges. Despite the uncertainty and unknowns of her life, she was confident and ready to take on the world.

SIX

Rohit's Rise in the UK : Journey to Success

Rohit couldn't believe his luck. He had come to the UK and was working for one of the most prestigious companies in the world. It was a far cry from his life in the suburbs of Mumbai, but he was determined to make the most of this opportunity. The days turned into weeks, and the weeks turned into months. Rohit worked tirelessly, putting in long hours and late nights, but he was determined to succeed.

One day, Rohit's boss called him into his office. "Rohit, I want to talk to you about your work," his boss said, looking sternly at him. Rohit's heart sank. He had been working so hard, and now he was afraid he had done something wrong.

"I'm pleased to tell you that your hard work has not gone unnoticed," his boss said, his expression softening. "We're promoting you to the position of Senior Manager, effective immediately."

Rohit couldn't believe what he was hearing. He had worked so hard for this moment, and now it was finally happening. He felt a surge of pride and accomplishment wash over him.

As Rohit left his boss's office, he couldn't help but think about his journey. From the small village near suburbs of Mumbai to the bustling streets of London, he had come a long way. He had faced countless obstacles along the way, but he had persevered. He knew that this was just the beginning, and he was excited to see where life would take him next.

As he walked out of the building, he felt the cool breeze on his face, and he smiled. He was living proof that hard work and determination could take you places you never thought possible.

As he reached his residence, Rohit couldn't help but reflect on how his hard work and dedication had paid off. He felt excited to see what other surprises life had in store for him.

Over the time, he quickly made a name for himself in the business world, and was soon sought after by other companies for his expertise and skills.

As his career took off, Rohit also made the most of his time in the UK, exploring the country and immersing himself in its rich culture and history. He visited museums and galleries, attended cultural events, and made new friends from all over the world.

Despite his busy schedule, Rohit never forgot his roots, and would often travel back to India to visit his family and friends. He remained connected to his culture, and was always eager to share his experiences and knowledge with those back home.

However, as much as he loved his life in the UK, Rohit always felt that something was missing. He longed for a deeper connection with someone, and often thought about settling down and starting a family of his own.

ღღღ

SEVEN

ROMEO MEETS JULIET: LOVE AT FIRST SIGHT

Rohit had always been fascinated by the United Kingdom and its rich culture and history. He was eager to immerse himself in a new culture and experience all that the UK had to offer.

In his free time, Rohit would explore the city, visiting museums, art galleries, and cultural events. He was fascinated by the beauty and diversity of London, and was always eager to learn more about the city and its people.

One day, Rohit decided to visit a local art gallery that was showcasing works by some of the most famous artists in the world. He was a passionate art lover, and was eager to see the masterpieces up close.

As he wandered through the galleries, taking in the stunning works of art, he suddenly found himself face to face with a beautiful young woman.

And Yes, that was Sarah, she was visiting the gallery with

her friends.

Rohit was immediately struck by Sarah's beauty and grace. She had a poise and elegance that was rare to find in this day and age. He couldn't take his eyes off her and decided to muster the courage to go and speak to her.

"Hi, I'm Rohit," he said, extending his hand.

"Hi, I'm Sarah," she replied, taking his hand and giving him a warm smile.

Both admiring the same painting. He glanced over at her and said, "That's a beautiful painting, isn't it?"

Sarah turned to him and smiled, "Yes, it is. I love how the colors blend together so seamlessly."

Rohit nodded in agreement, "The artist is incredibly talented."

They started talking more about the painting and art in general. As they walked around the gallery, they found themselves drawn to each other. Rohit couldn't help but feel a connection with Sarah, and he knew he had to find a way to see her again.

Finally, as they reached the end of the exhibit, Rohit said, "Would you like to grab a coffee with me? We could continue our conversation."

As it happening in the bollywood movies, our heroine Sarah also smiled and agreed, and they walked to a nearby café. As they sipped their coffee and talked, Rohit couldn't help but feel like he had known Sarah for a long time. They shared stories about their lives, their hobbies, and their interests.

Finally, as they finished their coffee, Rohit said, "Sarah, I know this might sound a bit forward, but I'd really like to see you again. Would you like to go out with me sometime?"

Sarah smiled and said, "I'd like that very much, Rohit."

And with that, Rohit and Sarah's love story began.

Sarah and Rohit exchanged numbers and made plans to see each other again. They were both eager to continue their conversation and learn more about each other.

It was one of those days that they kept meeting, Rohit and Sarah were sitting at a coffee shop, enjoying a warm cup of tea on a chilly afternoon. Rohit looked at Sarah with a curious gaze and asked, "Hey, Sarah, can you tell me about your early life?"

Sarah hesitated for a moment before responding, "Sure, I can. I grew up in a pure conservative but somewhat rich family in the UK. My parents were strict, and we followed traditional customs and practices. We didn't have many modern amenities at home though we are rich enough to get those, and our family time was mainly focused on religious activities and cultural events."

Rohit listened intently and asked, "How did you feel about that growing up? Did you ever wish things were different?"

Sarah sighed, "To be honest, it was challenging at times. I often felt like I didn't fit in with my peers at school who were more modern and progressive. I wasn't allowed to date, attend parties or have a social life outside of school, which made it hard for me to make friends."

Rohit looked at her sympathetically and asked, "Did you ever rebel against your family's strict rules?"

Sarah shook her head, "No, I never did. My family was very strict, and I didn't want to disappoint them. I respected their beliefs and values, even though it was difficult for me at times."

Rohit nodded in understanding and asked, "How did you meet Rubi then, if you weren't allowed to have a social life outside of school?"

Sarah smiled, "I met Rubi in school, and we became friends because we shared similar interests in academics and literature. Even though we couldn't hang out outside of school, we found ways to connect and stay in touch."

Rohit smiled back at Sarah and said, "You're a strong person, Sarah. Your upbringing has made you who you are today, and I admire you for that."

Despite their different backgrounds and cultures, Rohit and Sarah quickly hit it off. They talked for hours, discussing their shared love of art and travel. Sarah was everything that Rohit had been searching for - she was kind, adventurous, and full of life.

As they talked, Rohit felt like he had known Sarah for years. They had an instant connection and shared a sense of humor that made them both laugh. They spoke about their passions and their dreams, and Rohit was impressed by Sarah's intelligence and passion for making a difference in the world.

Over the next few weeks, Rohit and Sarah saw each other regularly, always finding new things to talk about and explore together. They soon became inseparable, and their relationship grew stronger with each passing day.

ϸϸϸ

EIGHT

LOVE IN THE LONDON CITY: ROHIT AND SARAH'S ROMANTIC DAYS

One fine day as the night wore on, Rohit found himself captivated by Sarah's beauty and charm. He knew that he had to see her again, and he mustered the courage to ask her out on a date.

"Sarah, I would love to take you out for dinner," Rohit said, hoping she would say yes.

Sarah smiled and nodded, and Rohit felt a rush of excitement. He knew that this was the start of something special.

They went on a romantic dinner date the following evening, and it was like they had known each other for years. They talked about everything under the sun, from their favorite books to their favorite foods.

As the night wore on, Rohit realized that he had found the one he had been searching for. He took Sarah's hand and looked into her eyes.

"Sarah, I know we've only known each other for two months, but I feel like I've known you for a lifetime. I don't want to spend another day without you in my life. Will you be my girlfriend?" he said, his heart pounding with anticipation.

Sarah smiled and nodded, and Rohit felt like the luckiest man in the world. He knew that this was the start of something beautiful, and he couldn't wait to see what the future held for them.

Rohit and Sarah's love had only grown stronger with each passing day, and their time in the UK was no exception. The new surroundings and cultural experiences brought a renewed excitement to their relationship, and they found themselves falling deeper in love every day.

From exploring the bustling streets of London to taking romantic walks in the countryside, Rohit and Sarah were never far from each other's side. They were a perfect match, complementing each other in every way, and their love was an inspiration to those around them.

One of their favorite things to do was to discover new restaurants and sample the local cuisine. They loved trying new foods and exploring the vibrant food culture of the UK, and they cherished the moments they spent together over a candlelight dinner or a cozy picnic in the park.

In the evenings, they would often attend the theater or visit local museums, taking in the rich cultural heritage of the UK. The art and architecture of the country left a deep impression on both of them, and they felt like they were discovering a whole new world with each other.

The couple also loved to travel and explore the countryside. They took romantic weekend getaways to quaint villages and historic castles, and they were constantly amazed by the natural beauty of the UK.

Despite their busy schedules, Rohit and Sarah made sure to set aside time for each other every day. They would often take long walks or sit together in quiet contemplation, simply enjoying each other's company.

And when they returned home at the end of the day, they would curl up together on the couch and share stories from their day, their love only growing stronger with each passing moment.

Their love was not only evident in their actions but also in the way they looked at each other. Their eyes would light up whenever they saw each other, and they were constantly touching and holding hands, a physical manifestation of the deep love and connection they shared.

Their relationship was a true fairy tale, a perfect union of two people from different worlds who had found each other and fallen deeply in love. They were a testament to the power of love, and their story inspired others to never give up on their own dreams of finding true love.

Years went by, and Sarah and Rohit's love continued to grow stronger with each passing day. They faced many challenges, but always remained steadfast in their commitment to each other. Through it all, they remained a true testament to the power of love, and a reminder that no matter where we come from, love knows no bounds.

As they celebrated their love and their life together in the UK, Rohit and Sarah knew that their love would only continue to grow and flourish in the years to come. They were deeply grateful for each other and for the love that they shared, and they were excited to see what the future held for them.

♡♡♡

NINE

Disapproval and Heartbreak: Sarah's Parents' Reaction to Her Love

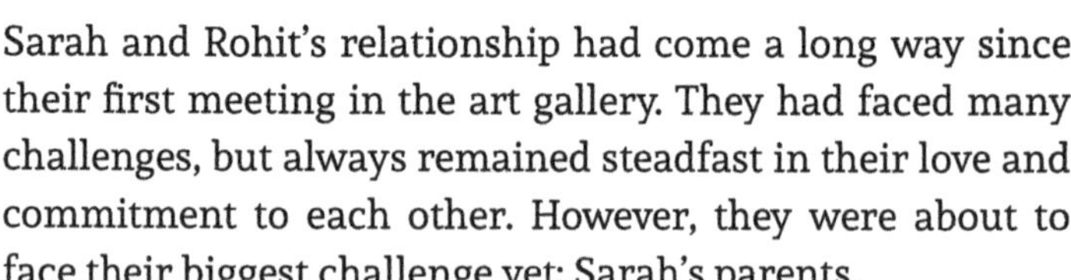

Sarah and Rohit's relationship had come a long way since their first meeting in the art gallery. They had faced many challenges, but always remained steadfast in their love and commitment to each other. However, they were about to face their biggest challenge yet: Sarah's parents.

Sarah's parents were traditional, conservative people who valued their British heritage and cultural values. They had high expectations for their daughter and wanted her to marry a man from a similar background. They were not prepared for the idea of Sarah dating someone from India, and were concerned about the cultural differences and the potential for conflict.

When Sarah first told her parents about Rohit, they were shocked and initially refused to accept the relationship. They believed that Sarah was making a mistake and that Rohit was not a suitable match for her.

"Sarah, are you sure about this? He's from a different background and culture than we are," her father said, concern etched on his face.

"I know, dad, but I love him. He makes me happy, and we share the same values and goals in life," Sarah replied, hoping to put her father's worries to rest.

Her mother chimed in, "But what about your future, Sarah? You know how important it is to marry someone who can provide for you and your family."

"I understand that, mom, but Rohit is successful and driven. He has a bright future ahead of him, and I believe in him," Sarah said, determination in her voice.

Despite Sarah's protests, her parents refused to listen, and the family was soon torn apart by their disagreement.

Sarah was heartbroken. She loved her parents deeply and did not want to hurt them, but she also loved Rohit and was determined to make their relationship work. She was torn between her love for her parents and her love for Rohit, and she did not know what to do.

***

Next day sarah came to Rohit's flat and explaining about her parents reaction. Both sat across from each other at their kitchen table, each with a cup of tea in hand. It had been a long day for both of them, and they were looking forward to some quiet time together.

Sarah sighed and leaned back in her chair. "You know, Rohit, sometimes I feel like we're from two different worlds. It's like we're speaking different languages."

Rohit nodded in agreement. "I know what you mean. It's hard for me to reconcile the expectations of your family with the reality of life here in the UK. And I know that sometimes my communication style can come off as abrupt or even rude."

Sarah reached across the table to take his hand. "I understand that, but sometimes it can be frustrating for me.

Rohit squeezed her hand. "I'm sorry that you feel that way, Sarah. It's important to me that we find a way to balance our cultural differences without sacrificing who we are as individuals."

Sarah smiled. "I agree. And I think that's why it's so important for us to talk about these things openly and honestly. We can't just sweep them under the rug and hope they go away."

Rohit nodded in agreement. "You're right. We have to work together to overcome these challenges. That's the only way we can build a happy and fulfilling life together."

As they finished their tea and cleared the dishes, Rohit and Sarah knew that their journey as a cross-cultural couple would have its ups and downs. But they were committed to facing those challenges together, with honesty, empathy, and a deep and abiding love.

Rohit, meanwhile, was equally heartbroken. He understood why Sarah's parents were concerned and did not want to cause any further conflict, but he also believed that love knows no bounds. He was willing to do whatever it took to win Sarah's parents over and make their relationship work.

Despite the challenges, Sarah and Rohit refused to give up on their love. They were determined to find a way to make their relationship work, and they began working together to bridge the gap between their cultures.

They started attending cultural events and workshops, learning about each other's heritage and values. They also made an effort to understand each other's families and backgrounds, and soon found that they had more in common than they had initially thought.

ꝒꝒꝒ

TEN

Rohit Breaking the News: Tells His Parents About Sarah and Love

Rohit had always been close with his parents, and he valued their opinions and guidance. However, he knew that telling them about his relationship with Sarah would be a difficult conversation. He was aware of the cultural differences between their families and was worried about how his parents would react.

Despite his concerns, Rohit knew that he had to be honest with his parents about his feelings for Sarah. He wanted their support and wanted to build a future with her, and he felt that he couldn't do that without the support of his family.

One evening, after dinner, Rohit gathered the courage to have the conversation with his parents. He sat down with them in the living room and took a deep breath before starting the conversation.

"Mom and Dad, I have something important to tell you," Rohit said. "I've been seeing someone, and I love her very much."

His parents looked at him with surprise, and his mother asked, "Who is she?"

"Her name is Sarah, and she's from England," Rohit replied.

There was a long silence, and Rohit could see the look of concern on his parents' faces. He could sense that they were worried about the cultural differences and the potential for conflict.

"I understand that this is difficult for you, but I want you to know that I love Sarah with all my heart," Rohit continued. "She is kind, caring, and supportive, and I believe that she is the one for me."

His parents looked at each other, and then back at Rohit. They were silent for a few moments, and then his father spoke.

"Rohit, we love you, and we want you to be happy," he said. "But we are worried about the cultural differences and the potential for conflict."

"I understand your concerns, but I believe that love knows no bounds," Rohit replied. "I am willing to work hard to make our relationship work, and I believe that Sarah and I can overcome any obstacles that come our way."

His parents were silent for a few moments, and then his mother spoke.

"Rohit, we are proud of you for being honest with us and for being so sure of your feelings," she said. "We will support you in your relationship with Sarah, and we will do our best to understand and accept your love for each other."

Rohit was overjoyed by his parents' response. He had expected a more difficult conversation, but he was grateful for their understanding and support.

Over the next few months, Rohit and Sarah worked hard to bridge the gap between their cultures and families. They attended cultural events and workshops, learning about each other's heritage and values. They also made an effort to understand each other's families and backgrounds, and soon found that they had more in common than they had initially thought.

Rohit's parents became more and more supportive of their relationship, and they saw the love and respect that Rohit and Sarah had for each other. They realized that their differences were what made their relationship so special, and they became proud of their son for finding such a wonderful partner.

Their relationship continued to grow stronger, and they were a shining example of the power of love and the strength of the human spirit. They were a true inspiration to all

ELEVEN

The Battle for Love: Rohit's Struggle to Win Over Sarah's Parents

Rohit's struggle to win over Sarah's parents was a long and difficult journey. Despite the love he felt for Sarah and the joy they brought each other, he knew that winning the approval of her parents would be no easy feat.

Sarah's parents were strict traditionalists, deeply rooted in their British heritage and wary of outsiders. They saw Rohit as a young man from a completely different world, with no understanding of their culture or way of life.

But Rohit was determined to show them the depth of his love for Sarah and his commitment to their future together. He knew that he would have to work hard to earn their trust and respect, but he was willing to do whatever it took.

Over the next few months, Rohit made a concerted effort to show Sarah's parents what he was made of. He threw himself into his work, determined to prove himself as a hardworking and responsible young man.

He also made a point of learning about the culture and traditions of the UK, reading books and speaking with local experts to deepen his understanding of the country and its people.

Despite his best efforts, however, Sarah's parents remained skeptical. They saw his actions as a mere show, and they remained convinced that he was not the right man for their daughter.

Rohit was undeterred. He knew that he would have to try even harder, and so he set his sights on proving himself in a more personal way.

He made a point of spending time with Sarah's parents, asking them questions about their lives and their culture and genuinely listening to their stories. Slowly but surely, he began to earn their trust, showing them the depth of his love for Sarah and his respect for their family.

It was a long and difficult journey, but Rohit's persistence paid off. Over time, Sarah's parents came to see him in a new light, recognizing the depth of his love for their daughter and the strength of his character.

Finally, on a warm summer evening, Sarah's parents summoned Rohit to their home for a formal meeting. When he arrived, they told him that they had been watching him closely and that they were impressed by his dedication and commitment.

Tears filled Rohit's eyes as he realized that his dream was finally within reach. With a deep sense of gratitude, he thanked Sarah's parents for their understanding and pledged his love and commitment to their daughter.

From that moment on, Rohit and Sarah's love was blessed by her parents, and the young couple was free to pursue their dreams together. They were a shining example of true love and commitment.

In the end, Rohit's struggle to win the hearts of Sarah's parents was a testament to the power of love and determination. He had proven that anything was possible, and he had shown the world what it truly meant to love someone with all your heart.

TWELVE

First Impressions: Sarah Meets Rohit's Parents

Rohit had been eagerly anticipating his parents' arrival in the UK for weeks. He had been counting down the days until he could finally introduce them to Sarah, the woman he loved more than anything in the world.

The day finally arrived, and Rohit was a bundle of nerves as he and Sarah greeted his parents at the airport. He was filled with a mixture of excitement and anxiety, unsure of how his parents would react to his British girlfriend.

Sarah was equally nervous, having never met Rohit's parents before. She had heard so much about them and was eager to make a good impression.

As they made their way back to the home, Sarah could sense the tension in the air. She tried her best to break the ice, making small talk and asking Rohit's parents about their journey.

But the tension only seemed to grow as they entered the home, with the silence in the room becoming almost palpable. Sarah could see the look of shock and confusion on Rohit's parents' faces as they took in the sight of their son's British girlfriend.

For what felt like an eternity, no one spoke. It was as if everyone was holding their breath, waiting for someone to make the first move.

And then, just as the silence was becoming unbearable, Rohit's mother finally spoke.

"Is this the girl you've been telling us about, Rohit?" she asked, her voice shaking with emotion.

Rohit nodded, taking Sarah's hand and holding it tightly.

"Yes, Mama. This is Sarah," he said, his voice filled with pride. "She's the love of my life, and I want you both to know her."

There was another long pause, and Sarah could feel her heart racing as she waited for Rohit's parents‘ reaction.

And then, to her surprise, Rohit's mother did something unexpected. She walked over to Sarah, took her hand in hers, and looked her in the eye.

"You're very beautiful, my dear," she said, her eyes filling with tears. "And we are so grateful to have you in our son's life."

Sarah was taken aback by the warmth in Rohit's mother's voice, and she felt tears prick at the corners of her own eyes.

"Thank you," she said, her voice trembling. "I love your son more than anything in the world, and I will do everything in my power to make him happy."

And with that, the tension in the room finally began to dissipate. Rohit's parents and Sarah spent the rest of the day talking and getting to know each other, their hearts filled with love and acceptance.

As the evening came to a close and Rohit's parents retired to their room for the night, Sarah and Rohit sat together on the couch, holding each other close.

"I can't believe it," Sarah whispered, her head resting on Rohit's shoulder. "Your parents are wonderful."

"I know," Rohit said, kissing the top of her head. "I'm so grateful they were able to see how much I love you, and how much you love me."

And with that, the couple snuggled up close, grateful for the love they shared and the support of their families. They knew that their future together would be filled with challenges, but with love and understanding on their side, they were ready to face anything that came their way.

♡♡♡

THIRTEEN

Bridging the Gap: The Meeting of Rohit and Sarah's Families

It was a day of high tension as Rohit and Sarah's parents gathered in the living room of Rohit's home. The two families had never met before, and the meeting was meant to decide the fate of Rohit and Sarah's relationship.

Rohit's parents sat on one couch, while Sarah's parents sat on another. The room was silent as they all waited for someone to speak. It was Rohit who broke the silence.

"Thank you for coming today," he said, looking at both sets of parents. "Sarah and I have something very important to tell you."

As you all know "We're in love," Sarah said, taking Rohit's hand.

There was a long silence as the two families took in what had just been said. It was Sarah's father who finally spoke.

"I have to be honest," he said. Eventhough i have accepted their love but still, "I have my concerns about this relationship."

Rohit's father nodded in agreement. "We understand your concerns," he said. "But we believe in our son, and we believe in his love for Sarah."

Sarah's mother spoke up. "I too have some concerns," she said. "But I also believe in the power of love, and I want to give them a chance."

The room was silent again as everyone considered what had been said. It was clear

that there were still many obstacles in the way of Rohit and Sarah's relationship, but they were both determined to overcome them.

"We want to make this work," Rohit said. "We're willing to do whatever it takes to show you that our love is real."

Sarah's father nodded, and Rohit's mother spoke up. "I have an idea," she said. "Why don't we all go out and have dinner together tonight? It will give us a chance to get to know each other and see if we can find common ground."

The room was filled with a sense of relief as everyone agreed to the plan. They all went to a local restaurant, and the atmosphere was surprisingly relaxed and comfortable. They laughed and shared stories, and by the end of the meal, it was clear that the two families were starting to bond.

Over the next few weeks, Rohit and Sarah's parents continued to spend time together, going on outings and attending cultural events. They began to understand each other's backgrounds and values, and they realized that they had much more in common than they had originally thought.

One day, after a particularly enjoyable outing, Sarah's father pulled Rohit aside. "I have to admit, I was skeptical at first," he said. "But I've come to see that your love for Sarah is real, and I want to support it."

Rohit's father nodded in agreement. "We're proud of our son," he said. "And we're grateful to Sarah and her family for giving us a

chance."

The two families hugged and celebrated their newfound understanding and acceptance of each other. It was clear that Rohit and Sarah's love was stronger than ever, and that their families were fully supportive of their relationship.

The decision to support Rohit and Sarah's love was a turning point for both families. They realized that despite their differences, they could find common ground and support each other. They proved that love knows no bounds and that with hard work and dedication, anything is possible.

Sarah and Rohit were ecstatic after their families approved of their relationship. After much discussion, they decided to have their engagement ceremony in London, where they had met and fallen in love. The event was to be a grand celebration, and both families spared no expense to make it a memorable occasion.

The love between Rohit and Sarah continued to flourish, and their families became close, supporting each other through thick and thin. It was a beautiful example of the power of love, the strength of the human spirit, and the importance of family.

FOURTEEN

The Engagement: A Celebration of Love

As the sun set on a balmy evening in London, the air was thick with the sound of music, laughter, and chatter. It was the day of Rohit and Sarah's engagement, a celebration of their love and commitment to each other.

The venue was decorated with fairy lights and flowers, the tables adorned with golden cutlery and pristine white napkins. Guests from both families had gathered to celebrate the union of Rohit and Sarah, their faces beaming with joy and excitement.

As the evening progressed, the couple made their way to the stage, hand in hand. The room hushed as they took the microphone, and Rohit spoke, his voice ringing out with sincerity and emotion.

"Today is a special day for Sarah and me. It is the day that we formally declare our love and commitment to each other, in the presence of our families and loved ones. I stand here today, proud and humbled, to call Sarah my fiancée. She has brought so much love, joy, and beauty into my life, and I cannot wait to spend the rest of my life with her."

As Rohit spoke, Sarah's eyes welled up with tears of joy, her heart overflowing with love for the man she was going to marry.

The evening was filled with laughter, music, and dance. Friends and family members took turns to congratulate the couple and offer their blessings. The dance floor was packed, and the DJ played hit after hit, keeping the guests on their feet.

During the ceremony, Rohit's family had one request - they wanted the wedding to take place in India, their homeland. Sarah and her family were a little apprehensive at first, but they eventually agreed. They knew how important it was for Rohit and his family to have the wedding in India.

After the ceremony, there was a lavish dinner and everyone danced the night away. It was a night to remember for both families, and they couldn't wait for the wedding in India.

As the night drew to a close, Sarah and Rohit were both filled with joy and gratitude, their eyes locked in a loving gaze. As they swayed to the music, they knew that their love had overcome all the obstacles and challenges that had come their way. They knew that they had each other, and that was all that mattered.

Despite the challenges of planning a wedding in a different country, both families were determined to make it happen. They started making arrangements immediately, and the wedding was scheduled to take place in a few months' time.

The engagement was a celebration of love, a testament to the power of two people who were determined to make their love story a reality. It was a day that would be etched in their memories forever, a day that marked the beginning of a new journey, a journey that they would take together, hand in hand.

♡♡♡

FIFTEEN

Wedding Bells in India: A Union of Two Cultures

The wedding day had finally arrived, and Rohit and Sarah were filled with emotions as they prepared to tie the knot.

It was a day of excitement and anticipation as the two families traveled to India for wedding. They arrived in the vibrant city of Mumbai, eager to experience the rich culture and traditions of India.

Rohit and Sarah's wedding was a true celebration of the union of two cultures. It was a day filled with love, joy, and excitement as the couple going to exchange their vows in front of friends and family from both India and the UK.

The wedding was held in Mumbai, India, in a beautiful outdoor ceremony surrounded by lush greenery and the sounds of nature. The families were greeted by a vibrant procession of drummers and dancers, and they were immediately struck by the energy and excitement of the city. They were taken to a beautiful hotel, where they would be staying during their visit.

The next few days were filled with a whirlwind of activity as the families prepared for the wedding. They visited local markets, trying on traditional Indian clothing and jewelry, and learning about the customs and traditions associated with the wedding ceremony.

One of the highlights of the trip was a visit to the famous Elephanta Caves, where they marveled at the ancient rock-cut temples and the breathtaking views of the Arabian Sea. The families also visited the Gateway of India, a historic monument that symbolizes the rich history and culture of Mumbai.

As the wedding day approached, the excitement reached a fever pitch. The setting was a perfect reflection of the couple's love for both India and the UK, and it was a fitting backdrop for the beginning of their new life together.

The sun was shining bright, and the colorful decorations adorned the wedding venue, creating an atmosphere of joy and happiness. A magnificent palace with lush gardens and sparkling fountains.

The families gathered at the wedding venue, as Sarah stepped out of the car in her beautiful red and gold wedding attire, she was overwhelmed with emotions. She took a deep breath, feeling nervous and excited at the same time. Her eyes scanned the crowd, searching for Rohit, the love of her life.

Rohit stood at the altar, dressed in a traditional Indian Sherwani, waiting eagerly for his bride. His heart was pounding, and he could barely contain his excitement. He had never felt so happy in his life.

The bride and groom looked stunning in their traditional Indian attire, and the love and joy they felt was palpable. The guests were dressed in a mix of traditional Indian and Western clothing, reflecting the diverse backgrounds of those in attendance.

The ceremony was a beautiful blend of Indian and British traditions, with elements of both cultures woven seamlessly into the celebration. There were traditional Indian rituals, such as the tying of the sacred thread, and Western customs, such as the exchange of rings.

As the ceremony began, the guests watched in awe as Rohit and Sarah made their way down the aisle, their eyes locked in a gaze filled with love and happiness. The couple exchanged vows in a touching ceremony, promising to love and cherish each other for the rest of their lives.

The rest of the day was a whirlwind of celebration, with music, dancing, and feasting.

The wedding feast was a true gastronomic delight, showcasing the finest and most delectable dishes of Indian cuisine. The aroma of spices and herbs filled the air, tempting the guests with the mouth-watering flavors. From the traditional biryani to the creamy butter chicken, the menu was a perfect blend of classic and contemporary dishes.

The appetizers were a mix of crispy samosas, tender chicken kebabs, and tangy chutneys, tantalizing the taste buds with their savory goodness. The main course featured an array of dishes, including the fragrant vegetable curry, the spicy lamb rogan josh, and the rich dal makhani, all served with hot and fluffy naan bread.

The dessert selection was equally impressive, with the melt-in-your-mouth gulab jamun, the creamy ras malai, and the refreshing mango lassi. The guests couldn't resist indulging in the delicious sweets, savoring each bite with delight.

The wedding feast was not just a celebration of love but also a tribute to the rich and diverse culture of India, reflected in the sumptuous and flavorful food that brought everyone together in joy and happiness.

As the sun began to set, Rohit and Sarah took to the dance floor for their first dance as a married couple. The guests looked on in delight as the couple swayed to the beat of a beautiful Indian love song, their love for each other shining bright for all to see.

The celebration continued late into the night, with guests from both India and the UK coming together to share in the joy of the day. There were speeches and toasts, laughter and joyful tears, and a feeling of unity and love that transcended borders and cultural differences.

In the end, Rohit and Sarah's wedding was a testament to the power of love and the beauty of cultural diversity. It was a celebration of their love and a symbol of the union of two cultures, and it would be remembered for years to come as a day of joy, love, and happiness.

ᑭᑭᑭ

The newlyweds returned to the UK as husband and wife, ready to begin their life together as a

testament to the power of love and the beauty of cultural unity. They would continue to honor both of their cultures, cherishing the traditions and customs that made them who they were, and inspiring future generations to celebrate the diversity that made the world a beautiful and rich tapestry.

♡♡♡

SIXTEEN

A New Beginning: Life After Marriage

Rohit and Sarah's life together after their marriage was a testament to their love and commitment. They settled into their new home in the UK, surrounded by the love and support of their families.

At first, they faced challenges as they adjusted to life together, but they approached each challenge with love and understanding. Sarah learned about the rich culture and traditions of India, and Rohit embraced the customs and culture of the UK.

As time went by, their love only grew stronger. They traveled the world together, experiencing new cultures and making memories that would last a lifetime. They also started a family, and the birth of their son only deepened their love and commitment to each other.

Years passed, and Rohit and Sarah's love only continued to grow. They faced many challenges along the way, but they always stood by each other, supporting and encouraging each other through everything.

ᑭᑭᑭ

It was a summer day, and Rohit's son Raj was sitting cross-legged on the floor of his childhood bedroom, when he stumbled upon his father's diary. It was an old, worn leather journal, filled with yellowed pages and the strong smell of history.

Raj had always been curious about his parents' love story, and as he thumbed through the pages of his father's diary, he felt a sense of excitement and awe.

The first pages were filled with tales of Rohit's early life in India, of the sights and sounds of his childhood, and of the love he felt for his family. But as Raj turned the pages, he came to a section that was different from the rest. It was filled with poems, letters, and passages about a girl named Sarah, a girl from the UK who had captured Rohit's heart.

Raj read on, completely absorbed in his father's words. He felt his heart racing as he read about their first meeting, about their struggles and triumphs, about the joy and pain of their love.

And as he read on, he felt a sense of goosebumps. He was filled with pride and admiration for his parents, and he felt a connection to them that he had never felt before. He could see the love that they shared, the love that had brought them together and sustained them through all the years.

As Raj read through the diary, he felt as though he was living through his father's love story. He could see the way their eyes met across a crowded room, feel the electricity of their first kiss, and experience the joy of their wedding day. He could feel the heartache of their families' opposition, and the triumph of their eventual acceptance.

And finally, he came to the end of the diary, to the last page, which was simply a simple statement of love: "My love for Sarah will endure for all time."

Tears rolled down Raj's cheeks as he closed the diary. He felt as though he had been given a gift, a window into the hearts of his parents and a glimpse into the power of true love.

From that day on, Raj cherished his father's diary, and he made it a point to share the story of his parents' love with anyone who would listen. He was filled with a sense of pride and wonder, knowing that he was the son of two people who had shared a love that was truly extraordinary.

Raj knew that he wanted to do something special to honor his parents' love story on their 25th anniversary. He would plan a celebration, something that would bring the whole family together to celebrate the love that had brought them all into existence. He couldn't wait to see the look on his parents' faces when they saw what he had in store for them.

♡♡♡

Epilogue

As Rohit and Sarah sat in their living room, holding hands, they reminisced about their journey of love, of how they had come so far from their different worlds and cultures, to be together.

Rohit reached for a photo album and they began to flip through pages filled with pictures of their wedding, their travels, their children, and their family gatherings. They laughed and shed a few tears, remembering the happy and sad moments they had shared.

As they turned to the last page, Rohit spoke softly, "Sarah, can you believe that in just two months, we will be celebrating our 25th anniversary?"

Sarah smiled and squeezed his hand, "I still remember the day you proposed to me, it feels like it was just yesterday."

Their son Raj, who had been listening to their conversation from the other room, walked in and sat beside them. He looked at the album with a sense of wonder and curiosity.

"Mom, Dad, I just finished reading your diary. I never knew about the struggles and challenges you both had to face to be together. It's amazing to see how your love story has stood the test of time," Raj said with a hint of emotion in his voice.

Rohit and Sarah exchanged a glance, both knowing the depths of their love and the hurdles they had to overcome to be together. They were proud of their love and what they had built together.

As they sat there in silence, a sense of contentment and gratitude washed over them. They were grateful for their love, their family, and for the memories they had created over the years.

The sound of laughter and chatter from the other room broke their silence, reminding them of the life they had built and the love that had sustained them. They smiled, knowing that their love story would continue to inspire and be cherished for generations to come.

The Unlikely Lovebirds: A Love Story Of Two Cultures

The outcome of the love story of Rohit and Sarah was nothing short of a fairy tale. Against all odds, their love had flourished, and their marriage had stood the test of time. They had become a shining example of true love, an inspiration to all who knew them.

Their love story was not just a story of two individuals, but it was a story of two cultures coming together. Rohit, an Indian boy, and Sarah, a UK girl, had broken down the barriers of language, religion, and culture, and had found love in each other.

Their marriage had brought their families together, and had created a bond that would last for generations to come. Their love story was an example of how love knows no bounds, and how it can bridge the gap between cultures and nations. They had shown the world that love is the strongest force of all, and that it has the power to bring people together, despite their differences.

The legacy of Rohit and Sarah's love story lived on, long after their time. Their children and grandchildren grew up with a deep appreciation for the rich cultural heritage of India, and for the love that their parents had shared.

In every generation, their story was passed down, becoming a part of the family's history, and a reminder of the power of love. It inspired new generations to follow in their footsteps, to break down barriers, and to find love in unexpected places.

***"The Unlikely Lovebirds: A Love Story of Two Cultures"** is a heartwarming tale of how love can transcend cultural differences and bring* *people together. It reminds us that no matter where we come from or what our background is, love knows no boundaries.*

ꕤꕤꕤ

Stay Connected: Follow The Author On Social Media

About Author

Parthasarathy G is an Engineering Graduate from Tamilnadu, India with more than a decade of exposure to the IT industry. In addition to his profession, he is passionate about studying everything about humanities, life, and Social science subjects. His books always talk about human life, good society, philosophy, and motivational things.

The author is currently living in Chennai, the capital city of Tamilnadu State and the gateway of the culture of South India.

ᑭᑭᑭ

If you're not already following me on Socialmedia, you can check out my accounts at below where I post about my books...

*Instagram : **@sarathycreations***

*Twitter : **@sarathy1210***

ᑭᑭᑭ

Reviews are crucial for independent authors like me, and would greatly appreciate your honest thoughts on our book. If you have a few minutes to spare, please consider leaving a review on [Amazon/Flipkart/Instagram/other platform].

Thank you for your support!

♡♡♡

Printed by Libri Plureos GmbH in Hamburg, Germany